THE BRAIN OF BRIAN

and other Telling Tales

Phil Jenkins

INTRODUCTION

Phil is telling tales.

A wide selection of short stories. Imaginative and humorous, covering a broad variety of topics from a brain transplant, to life through the eyes of one very clever and sophisticated seagull.

Feel the terror a young pilot trying to escape from a shot up Spitfire in the Battle of Britain, share the experience of a couple trying to escape the attentions of a rutting Stag in Bushy Park, or help save the life of an injured vulture in South America.

From dark humour, tense drama to light hearted and feel good, these stories have it all for you to enjoy.

Phil concludes with a true account of his early days in Persia and Ecuador.

CONTENTS

The Brain of Brian 6

    Set in the not to distant future, when brain .transplants are a reality, this story has elements of dark humour about the consequences. How would you feel if your lover came back with a different brain? (Contains adult material).

Nicholas Livingston Seagull 18

    Nick is one sophisticated seagull. He prefers his fish fried instead of cold and raw out of the sea, and preferably with an ice cream dessert. Could this be the result of a previous life?

Spitfire Experience 22

    A young pilot struggles for his life in the battle of Britain. So young and so talented. Trapped in a flying coffin.

Pecker 29

    A vulture can make a great pet. Well probably not, but it can show gratitude, even love? Shirley knows it can.

A Stag in the Park 35

A pleasurable walk, on a sunny day from Teddington lock to Hampton Court Palace, ends abruptly at Bushy park.

High Dining 40

High altitude food and highly priced wine proves a successful combination in this sky high experience.

Imagine a Number 44

Do you know what is real from what's imaginary. After all two negatives do make a positive. Don't they?

Cedric 46

Jenny came home to Paul to find Cedric in their bedroom, but Jenny's order for Paul to murder Cedric shocked Paul.

You Have Control 53

But what if he hasn't? A momentarily misjudgement could prove fatal for all of them, but who's fault was it?

Unseen Revenge 58

> What would you do if you could become invisible. Would you use your superpower responsibly?

Damaged 61

> Sometimes Charles' behaviour couldn't be described as normal. Could this be the result of his childhood with a dominant mother?

Nothing 64

> Is there life after death, or is that it?

Living in Lanzarote 66

> An account of life on the island of Lanzarote which includes tips to help you drive like a local!

Lost Childhood 72

An actual autobiographical account of the Author's childhood in Persia and Ecuador.

THE BRAIN OF BRIAN

Brian knew that he was about die and it is to be the most gruesome death. His parachute had been blown off course and he is descending into the fast rotating blades of a helicopter on it's landing pad.

The horrific scene was witnessed by a number of people, including two members of an organ recovery unit that was stationed nearby. Everyone watched, helpless to prevent the inevitable. Like fruit in a blender. A mush of blood and guts exploded and shredded body parts were being propelled in all directions. Brian was decapitated and his head shot into the air where it became entangled with the sinking parachute and landed on the grass. Brian's final view of this life was his flight in the air as his optic nerves sent their last messages to his brain. The organ recovery unit retrieved his head and performed a stabilisation.

*

Helen sat by Ted's bed in a private room in the National Hospital for Neurosurgery in London. Ted had suffered major brain damage as a result of late diagnosis of a brain tumour. He was in a vegetative state, in an induced coma and on life support. She looked at his beautiful face and remembered his perfect body as she recalled those fabulous times of love making and the feeling of absolute security as he would hold and cuddle her. Ted was the love of her life, her soul mate, her life. Now he lay here, body fine, but brain dead. She felt helpless and so alone.

She remembered that today was King William's 60th birthday and she pictured Ted raising a glass to him. Ted was a royalist at heart and as well as his many interests and talents, he was a concert pianist. He had met the King when he was invited to play at the Royal Variety Performance.

A doctor interrupted her thoughts as he entered the room. He told her that now there was hope. A good chance that everything would be alright. A compatible donor had been found. As a result of a tragic accident, the brain of Brian was being rushed to the hospital and the surgeons were preparing the operating theatre for a brain transplant.

*

Sarah opened the front door to be faced with two police officers with serious faces asking if she was the wife of Brian Jameson.

"What is it? What's happened?" She cried?

"Could we please come in?"Asked the officers, as Sarah nearly collapsed with a sinking feeling of dread.

Later, Charlotte answered the phone to a distraught Sarah, who broke the terrible news to

Brian's mother.

*

Helen was back at Ted's bedside. The operation went without problems and seemingly was successful. Helen was told the whole sad story about Brian. She contacted Sarah and Charlotte and invited them to the hospital to be at Ted's bedside when he was awoken from his induced coma which would be in about 72 hours.

As they all gathered at his bedside. Helen with her Father Dave and Sarah with Brian's Mother, Charlotte, the doctor initiated the final stage of Ted's return to conciousness. Helen studied her beloved Ted's face. All waited anxiously looking for signs of the return to life. Eventually, there was a flicker of eyelashes and Brian opened Ted's eyes. Then with eyes wide open, he looked around at Helen, Sarah, Charlotte and Dave gathered at his side and his face altered as he showed recognition.

"Sarah, Mum," he muttered.

"No Ted. You're Ted. My Ted," Helen cried inconsolably.

The next day Helen and Dave visit the hospital on their own.

"You are Ted. You are the man that married my daughter," said Helen's Father looking down at the sleeping patient.

"My beautiful Ted," sobbed Helen. "I love every inch of his body." "His passport says he's Ted, his driving licence says he's Ted, how can he think that he is Brian?"

The sound of voices wakes him and he opens his eyes. "Hi Ted", says Helen gently."

"Hello Helen," he responds. "Where is Sarah?" he asks with a soft southern Irish accent, which is strange to Helen. But it is definitely Ted's voice with the tones that she recognises.

"She's nearby, she will be here soon. Ted this is Dave, my Father. Your Father-in-law."

"No, I am Brian. I am married to Sarah", Brian protests.

Helen takes a mirror out of her handbag and holds it to his face.

"No, you are Ted, you are married to me."

Brian can't hide his confusion as Ted looks back at him in the mirror.

"Ted, I have arranged for a private convalescent suite for you and you are being moved there today. You will be up and about and able to come home in no time".

Before Brian can respond, the door opens and Sarah appears.

"Hello Brian, sweetheart, it's great that you are recovering so well. The doctor says that you could be home in a matter of weeks."

Then acknowledging their presence; "Hi Helen, Hi Dave. How are you both?"

"I will be better when I get Ted home", Helen retorts.

*

After a week in the comfort of his own convalescence suite, Brian is finding his feet and other parts of his new body. He is about to have his first shower and his admiring his naked body in the mirror. This is definitely an upgrade, he thinks.

In the shower, he begins to explore himself and becomes aroused. It is a very weird sensation, and he feels like he is playing with someone else. But this is all mine, he thinks as he grips his rock solid erection and beams with his intense pleasure of it's size. His excitement rises and rises and he comes with a super spurt that shoots a very satisfying distance. He is very pleased with the functioning of his new body and can't wait to try it out for real.

Both Sarah and Helen had visited him every day over the past week. Thankfully not together, as they competed for his time and attention.

Brian has been happily married to Sarah for five years and he couldn't imagine life without her. Although lately, something seemed to be wrong. Their love making was loosing it's intensity and Brian thought that he was not pleasing her and this caused him to be anxious, which only made matters worse. Despite Sarah's reassurances, their lovemaking became less and less frequent as they both became reluctant to initiate it.

Now Brian was sure, being confident with his new body, that he could sort that problem and was looking forward to trying. But, it was worrying, that he perceived that Sarah was having problems coming to terms with the new Brian.

Before the accident, they were planning to find somewhere larger than their small flat in

Ealing, so that they could start a family. But to afford that, they would have to move further out of town or relocate completely. Brian thought that now, there might be problems with his present job and this could be the factor that decides the relocation, but he knows that Sarah loves her job and she isn't convinced.

*

Helen was in love with Ted, she loved his body and she is becoming to accept and like Brian. She visited him whenever she could and they were becoming good friends. Brian had to admit to himself that he looked forward to her seeing her. She was vivacious and very attractive and she obviously loved the pants off his body. She told him that they were fantastic together in bed and if he didn't remember that, she could refresh his memory.

He had learned from her, that he was a concert pianist, who lived in a large house with an indoor swimming pool in Esher and that he drove an Aston Martin. Helen made it clear that she wanted him to come home with her and all this would be his. She left him with a kiss on the lips that Brian didn't resist. Brian is becoming of two minds.

*

Two days before he is due to leave hospital and return home. Brian is sitting in his suite awaiting an appointment with a legal counsellor. There is a knock at the door and in walks Sylvia. She is slim with a pretty face and dressed in a smart, business-like black skirt and jacket. Brian guesses she is in her mid thirties. She is very personable and pleasant and easily engages Brian in conversation and asks questions to access his situation and his intentions. She tells Brian that under the Transitions and Changes Act 2038, he must register with the Department of Births, Deaths, Marriages and Changes and that she has the forms with her, if he wishes to do so today.

She explains that he has the legal right to choose whether he be Brian Jameson or Ted Willis. If he chooses to be Ted, he is legally married to Helen and can continue to use his Passport and driving licence etc. without change. If he chooses to be Brian, he is legally married to Sarah and must apply for a new passport, driving licence and any other document that requires a photo ID.

He is advised that in registering, any criminal record or impending prosecutions for either party will remain on his record, but as there are none known for either Ted or Brian, that doesn't seem to be a problem.

If he chooses to be Ted. Sarah must register the death of Brian and if he chooses to be Brian, Helen must register the death of Ted.

Sylvia paused. Asked if he understood and if he had any questions. Then she said;

"So who are you going to be: Ted Willis or Brian Jameson?"

"Thanks Sylvia. But, that's a no-brain-er. I am Brian and I am happy to register that fact today."

*

Brian, now back with Sarah in their flat, is content with another quiet night in, as he is still adjusting to his new body. He is now taller, still slim but much better built and his hands and feet are slightly larger. All his shoes and clothes are now redundant and Helen was not offering anything of Ted's.

Brian remembers everything as it was: Sarah, his home, his seat on the sofa and his side of the bed and it gives him a feeling of security which he really needs now. He would be totally relaxed with everything, if it wasn't for Sarah behaving differently towards him.

Brian reaches out for his glass of red wine and the end of his finger flips the glass and sends it flying onto their new beige carpet.

"Not again," snaps Sarah.

Brian feels inadequate to express his frustration with himself. "Sorry," he says, "I just ...."

"No, I'm sorry," Sarah interrupts. "I am not being very patient, am I?"

Brian did think that she could be a bit more supportive and that things between them were not as he would want or expect, but he said;

"I understand and I will try and concentrate more on what I am doing. It's just that I misjudge things sometimes. It will be alright soon." Brian wasn't so sure that all will be right soon. Lovemaking with Sarah and his new body hadn't turned out to be as enjoyable as he thought it would be. Brian was confident that it would now be great and was full of desire and passion, but Helen wasn't as responsive as he had hoped. She was a virgin when she married Brian and it felt to her as if she was sleeping with another man. She couldn't reconcile this new body with Brian and this was causing anxiety and she found that she couldn't relax and enjoy it. All in all Brian's new life was turning out to be a disappointment.

When it came to Brian's first day back at work, Sarah got up early to make him breakfast and wish him well. Brian was an air traffic controller and wasn't sure what was in store for him today. He had a nine o'clock meeting with David Hardy who was his boss's boss. Brian was full of trepidation as he doubted whether he would still be able to do his job. But he reassured himself with the fact that he thought the same about whether he would be able to drive a car. A task that he managed instinctively, without any problems. Brian kissed Sarah goodbye and headed off on his old familiar journey to Heathrow.

As he drove through the tunnel, his stomach was churning. He didn't know how is old colleagues were going to react to the new Brian and dreaded it. He was tempted to turn back and just phone in his resignation; but no, he decided, he would force himself to do this.

When he arrived at his old place of work, he tried to avoid everyone and headed straight for David's office. He went past reception and headed for the lifts. But he was pursued by Susan, on reception, who called after him,

"Excuse me, can I help you?" She rushed up to him and asked "are looking for someone, can I help you?"

"I have an appointment with David Hardy."

"I'll have to phone it through", said Susan.

"No, it's all right Susan, it's Brian."

"I beg your pardon!"

"I am Brian. Brian Jameson," and he showed her his old security pass with a photo of the old Brian on it.

Susan had heard of what had happened to Brian and had been pre-warned to expect him, but it didn't lessen the shock. She stared, open-mouthed and looked Brian up and down. Wow, what a hulk she thought. Brian was never like this. She noticed that Brian was staring back at her, as if he was reading her thoughts and she blushed.

"I'll have to escort you to Mr. Hardy's office," she said.

The meeting with David was very strained. David treated him as if he was a stranger. Brian learned that he could not have his job back. He had to go on a probational period of re-training and assessment and then a decision will be made as to his future.

Brian left feeling deflated. He wasn't sure if he wanted to go through with this. Brian thought it would be better to move home and start again, but he knew that Sarah wouldn't agree to it. Brian was so down, he needed support. He wanted to be comforted.

When he got back to his car. Brian hunched forward over the steering wheel and sighed. Then he phoned Helen. She was very understanding and told him to come over.

"I am just half an hour down the road," she said "and I would love to see you."

Helen answered the door with a big smile and a hug. She was wearing a very short skirt with a blouse with that extra button unbuttoned.

"Great to see you looking so well. Come in, have a seat. Can I get you a glass of wine?"

"Thanks Helen, just what I need", said Brian as he took a seat on the enormous "L" shaped sofa.

"Take your jacket off, make yourself comfortable," said Helen while she poured two large glasses. She gave one to Brian as she sat down beside him and asked how he had been.

Brian started to pour his heart out and Helen was sympathetic and tender and comforted him. She moved close to him and kissed him gently on the lips and Brian responded. She started to unbutton his shirt and Brian didn't need any more encouragement. He had already been glancing down her blouse and was imagining her without it.

There followed a frantic removal of clothes. Helen making sure they were all off. Here was the body she craved for and she couldn't keep her hands off him. Brian thought Helen looked beautiful naked. She had a stunning body, but when he made a move to hold her, she pushed him so he lay on his back. She slid her hands down his chest. She was taking control and Brian didn't mind a bit. She held him and he quickly became aroused. She dipped her fingers into her wine glass and dripped some wine over the end of his erection and then licked she licked it off.

"I love sucking cock," she declared as she went down on him. This woman is wild, thought Brian and he wasn't complaining. Then she jumped on top and mounted him. Brian decided that she must be an accomplished rider and his excitement was reaching new levels, as the trot turned into a canter. Brian, loving every second was praying for it to last. Helen was groaning with pleasure, as Brian's excitement was reaching the point where he could hold back no longer. Then Helen let out a last, long ecstatic groan, just as Brian released. The tumultuous, trembling, joyous sensation of simultaneous orgasms took a little time to subside.

After which, Helen pleaded, "come and live with me, I can make you very happy."

Brian panted back; "Oh yes, yes I am sure you can, you really can, and Helen tell me."

"Yes Brian, what?"

"Have you still got the Aston Martin?"

NICHOLAS LIVINGSTON SEAGULL

I am Nicholas Livingston Seagull and like my Father Jonathan, I have been human in a previous existence. I am one super smart seagull. I have had many previous lives and being a seagull is great. Flying is just the most amazing fun experience and I do it well. I work out and practice and I can soar high, dive fast, hover accurately and swoop and glide effortlessly.

Believe me when I tell you, that compared to some of my lives, this is up there with the best. Definitely the worse was being a woodlouse. Fortunately, it didn't last long, just one day before I was trodden on.

I enjoy living in Cornwall amongst the many idyllic coastal fishing towns. The locals in St. Ives (that's the human locals, not my mates) call me Naughty Nick. Not because they know my name is Nicholas, but because I nick food from the tourists. This is an art that I have perfected.

Just look out there to sea, there are a flock

of my friends enthusiastically and noisily flying around a fishing boat in pursuit of fish morsels. What a waste of effort, all of them in the same place fighting over the same scraps. It's cold and wet and so are the fish.

I prefer mine warm and battered with chips. While they are all out to sea, getting tired and hungry, I am clever. I just find some tourists sitting on the seawall, enjoying their fish and chips in the sunshine and I fly down and perch next to them and give them a hungry gaze. They will usually throw me a chip or two and maybe a piece of fish, which I will entertainingly gobble up.

These are the nice people who enjoy feeding me and I appreciate them and take no more than they offer me. However, there are those who don't want to encourage us seagulls and would probably have us culled, if they had their way. To these people a different tactic is required. Again, I fly down and perch near them and give them my longing hungry look and if they don't respond and give me some food, I will fly around them and land on their shoulder. They will jump up and in fright and drop the their food and I will make off with a nice piece of fish or whatever takes my fancy. Works every time.

After my fish and chips, I usually like an ice cream. Not strawberry though, I prefer chocolate or coffee. I usually use the ice cream shop on the sea front. If you sit outside on the wall, you can see who is going in and what they are buying. I watch for someone taking some delicious brown ice cream.

Then it's a short flight up to the awning over the front of the shop and watch for them coming out, just under me. Then just a quick swoop down behind them grabbing the ice cream and away with it to somewhere pleasant, to savour my dessert.

Life here is very enjoyable. It not just eating well, but the surroundings are beautiful and there is plenty of entertainment.

One of my favourite ideas for fun is a flight along the coast up to Manor farm, where every Sunday you will find old Tom, the farm owner, polishing his beloved red sports car. Just as he finishing the final shine and stepping back to admire his work, I would test my skill and accuracy with a swift swoop over the car on a bombing run. Splat, splat all across the bonnet. Spot on. It drives him crazy and I fly off leaving Tom tamping.

A week later, perched on the end of the harbour wall, I am thinking to myself that it's been a great week. The weather has been glorious and the food abundant and varied. Yesterdays prawns off the buffet in the beer garden of the Jolly Sailor were particularly fine. I think I'm in the mood to take a flight up to Manor farm.

It's a warm sunny day and I am enjoying soaring and gliding along the coast. When I get there, I am surprised that there is no sign of Tom, but the car is there and it looks newly polished and as a bonus, the roof is down revealing his immaculate cream leather seats. I swoop down and with great skill drop two deposits across the seats and then perch on the wall by the barn. It's not so much fun not having Tom around to react to my performance. I was wondering where he could be, when a glint of sunlight on steel caught the corner of my eye. I turned, too late to avoid the discharge of two barrels aimed in my direction.

Now my sun has gone dark, my earth damp and cold. Oh no, I am a woodlouse again.

SPITFIRE EXPERIENCE

The childhood genius. Excelled in all subjects. Praise and admiration from all quarters. The offer of a place in Trinity College, Cambridge. It all now seemed a distant memory to this young man.

How the hell did he get here. This was never his plan. He was full of dread that this moment would come. Lately, with recent events, he thought about it more and more. Only this morning, he thought that his time would come soon, just as it had for so many close to him. Would he panic, would he cope, or would he die?

Now, his worst nightmare had become a reality. He raised his eyes to the red toggle hanging just above him. He knew exactly what he had to do and however difficult it seemed to him before, now in his present situation, it seemed virtually impossible. Even with all the training he had received, he had never done it for real and now was unsure whether he could actually do it. This was nothing like it was in the drill. But he had no choice, there was no alternative. Literally, do or die.

He tried to calm himself and focus his mind on the sequence of actions required to survive: Pull the red toggle down sharply to release the bolts of the canopy. Hit the quick release on the seat belts, remove his mask. Then push the canopy upwards with hands and elbows to jettison it. With your left hand on the throttle and right hand on the control stick, put the plane in level powered flight and while applying more throttle, move the stick sharply to the right to roll the plane on to its back, drop out of the seat and when clear of the plane pull the parachute release. Oh and by no account attempt to just climb out of the plane, because you will probably hit the tail on your exit, or worst, get your parachute entangled with the rear of the canopy or the tail and be dragged down with the plane to certain death.

So that's what he has to do. It's been drummed into him. But now in combat, with all eight of his Browning machine guns expired and with oil spewing from the damaged Merlin engine, his shot up Spitfire was filling with smoke and worst, there were flames coming from the front of the cockpit near the fuel tank, which was still half full, with about 40 gallons of fuel. Nothing in his short life had challenged him like this. This is the first time he has experienced a feeling of inadequacy and real fear.

Now thinking out loud Ron tried to motivate himself,

'Focus, focus as you have never done before. There has been nothing in your life that has been as important as the next few minutes. You can do this. Concentrate. Now pull that damn toggle!'

Ron tugged the toggle with determined force. He heard the reassuring clunk of the bolts releasing. He hit the release of his seat belts and removed his mask. He tried to push up and jettison the canopy but it wouldn't budge. Taking his hands off the stick had caused the damaged plane, which was now out of trim, to lurch and roll to the right. He grabbed at the stick and gained control, but things were not normal and it needed constant pressure on the stick, pushing to the left to maintain level flight. The cockpit was filling up with smoke and he was choking. He used his leg to keep the stick straight, while again pushing on the canopy with all his strength, but with no avail. The plane was losing airspeed and altitude. The engine was spluttering and vibrating and not firing on all cylinders. He pushed the throttle forward, through the gate, in a last attempt to extract power. With the last stuttering spurge of power, he pushed the control far right and rolled the plane upside down. Without his belts he fell on the canopy in a last ditch attempt to release it. The canopy held firm. The plane was now out of control, and the visibility in the cabin was decreasing due to the smoke. The control had a strong a bias to the right and the plane completed the barrel roll. Ron fell back into his seat. Now the nose was down and the plane was losing altitude rapidly, the throttle rammed forward was not generating any more power and he was loosing airspeed. He was going down. His stomach wrenched. Panic set in.

'Please! I don't want it to end like this.'

His mind raced. What now, for God's sake think. Then, instead of trying to pull the nose up with limited power, Ron pushed the joystick forward which caused the aircraft to go into a deep dive and then with full throttle and using the increased airspeed of the descent, he pulled the stick back to get out of the dive and achieve a momentary climb. Then, instead of pushing the stick to the right as he did before, he slammed it hard to the left against the bias and as the plane barrel rolled to the left. He took it past 180 degrees and he fell again hard against canopy. Deducing that the bias would return it to the upside down position, which it did, and as it did he forced his shoulders against the canopy and using his feet, gave one last almighty kick at the seat now above him, forcing his shoulders against the canopy, on which he was resting, which finally broke free and flew from the plane and Ron fell from cockpit. The sheer relief was momentous. So much so that he momentarily forgot to pull the release on his parachute, as he watched his Spitfire's last spiral descent to oblivion and the explosion as it landed on the South Downs below.

His parachute opened, without further problem and his descent was gentle but quick and he landed on, what now appeared to him as the glorious, green and pleasant, land of Sussex on the the most beautiful sunny August day that he had ever experienced. He felt himself shaking with a cocktail of emotions and exhaustion, but miraculously, with no pain. He checked himself over. He was intact, unhurt and alive, but with just one minor embarrassing problem. His trousers were wet. Oh god, he had pissed himself. He chuckled to himself, thinking that he would probably leave that detail out when recalling his tale, which surely he would. Then he laughed out loud. Hysterical laughter of relief, as with second thoughts, perhaps he would leave it in, explaining that it was a result of trying to put out the cockpit fire.

***

Seventy eight years later, in August 2018, Mike is visiting the RAF Museum in Hendon. He is there with his wife as part of his seventy second birthday celebration. He has a ticket for the "Spitfire Experience".

As he climbs into the cockpit he is filled with mixed emotions and a feeling of claustrophobia as he squeezes himself down onto the seat. He imagines what it must have like, as a young man, flying one of these things in the "Battle of Britain". He thought of the fear and dread that he would probably be feeling if it was him. It was a flying coffin and there was probably more room in a coffin.

He listened attentively to the young man instructing him as to the function of the controls and instruments and the history of the Spitfire since it was first manufactured by by the Supermarine Aircraft Company in 1936. How it was powered by a Rolls Royce Merlin engine and equipped with eight 0.303 Browning machine guns. As Mike takes the controls, he is talked through the take-off procedure and he becomes aware of how difficult that must have been without any visibility to the front, due to nose pointing skywards. The engines were extremely noisy and it would have been very hot, so you didn't close the canopy until the last minute before take off. You push the throttle with your left hand and keep it straight on the runway using the pedals. At 40mph the tail rises and you can see in front of you for the first time. With throttle fully forward, you pull back on the joystick and at 90mph you take off. When up in the air, you take your left hand off the throttle and hold the joystick, and with your right hand, now free, you raise the undercarriage and the wheels fold neatly under the plane as you soar skywards. Mike knows all this, but says nothing.

Then the young instructor starts to tell Mike about the emergency bail out procedure.

But Mike couldn't contain himself any more and interrupts him:

'I pull the red toggle, hit the belt quick release, take off my mask, push upwards on the canopy to jettison it, fly the plane upside down and drop out.'

The instructor gives him an intrigued smile,

'How do you know that?'

'My Father told me, he actually did it for real.' and then he added, 'he also told me how you put out a fire in the cockpit.'

PECKER

Shirley was suddenly apprehensive. The strange sounds seemed to coming from outside the fence of her yard. She cautiously opened the tall wooden gate and looked up the track leading to the road, where she saw two young boys tormenting a large bird. Shirley didn't hesitate to go to it's defence and shooed the boys away.

The bird cowered between the tree and the fence and stared up at her. Now, she thought, what am I going to do with you. This was one big ugly bird, but it was obviously in distress with a damaged foot and buckled wing and Shirley was not one to leave an injured animal to suffer. The trouble was that this bird was over two and half feet tall, it was black with a scary, sharply hooked beak, with a bald red head and fearful staring eyes. It looked liked a gigantic ugly turkey.

She had seen these before, the locals called them Gyanasers, they were a type of vulture and not the friendliest of creatures. Shirley pondered what to do. She didn't think that there were any vets around here and even if there was one, how was she going to get this creature there.

First she thought, let's get you somewhere safe. She went back through her yard into the kitchen, quickly cut up some pieces of meat and returned to the bird which was still exactly where she left it. She threw a piece of meat at it's feet which it hungrily gobbled up. Then she backed up a few feet and dropped another piece of meat. The bird half limped, half hopped forward and devoured the meat. She repeated this process until she had successfully enticed the bird into her yard.

She noticed that it was missing a toe on it's right foot and it didn't look like it could fly because it's right wing seemed damaged. She closed the gate of the yard, bolted it and then opened a door to one of the out-houses. She then threw some meat in through the open door. The bird looked at it, but didn't go in and looked at her suspiciously.

She had an idea that it would help it, if she could bathe it's foot and straighten it's wing, but the the look of that beak and those claws deterred her. Shirley dropped another piece of meat at it's feet and that was also quickly eaten. Then she had a thought and went into the house and came out again wearing a pair of gardening gloves and very slowly approached the bird. It hopped backwards against the wall of the shed. "Come on bird", she said "I am not going to hurt you" and very gently she put out her hand towards it, moving very cautiously. The bird tensed, it's neck stiffened, it's head went back and it's eyes gave a warning glare.

Shirley thought better of it. Time for plan B. Except she didn't really have a plan B. She decided to leave it alone for now and returned to the house.

She also decided that more meat was required, so she set out to drive into town in search of some. She would get some scrag ends and off-cuts for it.

Later returning with plenty of meat, she cut some up and placed it in a bowl and took it out for the bird, which was still in the yard. She noticed that the piece of meat, that she had thrown into the out-house had gone, so she concluded that it had ventured inside, which she thought was a good sign. She threw it another piece of meat that it gratefully ate and then showed it the bowl and placed it inside the out-house. The bird was still reluctant to go in. Finally she filled the trough outside with water and went back into the kitchen. She watched from the kitchen window as the bird timidly ventured into the out-house. Shirley was happy that she was making progress.

Later that evening when Joe, her husband, returned from work, she enthusiastically told him the story. Joe was amused and supportive of her helping this unfortunate creature. He loved her soft and caring nature. However, he was not quite so amused when she confessed that she had fed his steak to the bird. It was chips and egg for him tonight.

Shirley was ashamed that she forgot to mention, that she had been out to get more meat for the bird and forgot to replace the steaks that she fed it with.

The following morning, they were woken up early, by a tapping on the kitchen door. Shirley got up and opened the door to find the bird pecking at it.

"Oh it's you pecking at my door. I suppose you want breakfast? You a look a bit perkier today. Fancy pecking at the door, that's clever. We will have to call you Pecker." Shirley chopped up some meat and filled his bowl. Pecker certainly had quite an appetite.

This continued for a few days. Then on the Sunday morning, as Joe and Shirley slept after a good Saturday night out ..... Peck, peck.....Peck, peck, peck.

Joe woke suddenly, "That bloody bird, doesn't it know it's Sunday!"

Shirley jumped out of bed, "Don't worry I'll sort him. You stay there, I'll bring you a coffee."

That day Joe and Shirley had discussions about Pecker. Shirley promised Joe that Pecker wouldn't effect him and she would do all the looking after that was required.

Later that evening when she went out to feed Pecker. She found him on the roof of the out-house.

"Good boy, how did you get up there?"

As soon as Pecker saw her, he jumped of the roof and lop-sidedly glided to her feet and looked up at her expectantly. He looked much improved, his right wing wasn't opening fully but it was working and he was walking again. She was happy that

Pecker was recovering.

When she told Joe, he said that was really great and perhaps the bloody thing would fly off now. Shirley thought that perhaps he would and that saddened her. She had got very attached to Pecker and looked forward to him pecking on the door when he was hungry. It was not everyone who had a pet vulture.

The next morning Shirley woke at the usual time, Joe was still asleep beside her. She lay on her back, slowly rejoining the awoken world. Then it dawned on her, there was no pecking. She rushed out of bed, through the kitchen and into the yard and there was no Pecker. She looked all around and he was nowhere to be found. She had mixed emotions, glad that he was able to fly away and she really hoped that's what he did and that he was safe, but sad that he was gone. She was going to miss him.

Joe tried to console Shirley.

"There wasn't a good bye", said Shirley.

"What did you expect him to do.. leave a thank you note" said Joe rather insensitively.

Shirley didn't think that comment was called for and toyed with idea of feeding Joe with the rest of Pecker's meat.

Shirley thought a lot about Pecker over the following week and Joe reassured her by telling her that she had saved him and thanks to her, he was alive and well somewhere.

The following weekend, Joe and Shirley were having a lie in, when they heard it. Peck, peck.......

peck, peck,peck. They both sat up and stared at each other in disbelief. Shirley was at the kitchen door in an instant with Joe right behind her. She couldn't open the door fast enough.

There, before them, was Pecker, missing a toe, but otherwise looking fine. He gazed upwards at them, then hopped backwards and stretched out his wings displaying an impressive six foot of wingspan. He let out a raucous cry and flew up high above them. Then with his wings raised in a "V" he soared around in wobbly circles, letting out a series of high pitched shrieks, before flying off into the distance.

Joe smiled at Shirley's astonishment.

"Well", he said "I think that was his thank you note".

A STAG IN THE PARK

Enjoying a beautiful sunny afternoon in late September, my partner and I are sitting on a bench at Teddington Lock. The lock is a picturesque and peaceful place which is great for a picnic or somewhere just to sit and watch the boats pass by. We were discussing the lock and my partner asks me if I know how long the lock has been here. I don't know so I ask my phone about the lock. It tells me that the first lock at Teddington was built in 1810 and was made of timber and was replaced in 1856 with the one that we have today. In 1904 the barge lock was added making it the largest lock system on the non-tidal Thames.

Isn't technology wonderful? It's like having your own personal guide!

We decided to go for a long walk to Hampton Court Palace through Bushy Park and see the deer. Leaving the lock, we crossed the Thames via the blue steel pedestrian bridge which offers a good view of the weir and the locks. Resisting the temptation of the Anglers and Tide End Cottage pubs we made our way up Teddington High Street with it's interesting selection of small independent retailers, numerous coffee shops and a great variety of interesting restaurants. In addition to the conventional British cuisine, you can choose from Italian, Chinese, Thai, Indian, and Spanish. Also it's worth mentioning that, during our stroll, we passed no less than six inviting pubs. During our many stays here, we have managed to eat and drink in most of them. When we got to Station Road, we turned left and when we arrived at the station, we went through it and over the bridge crossing the railway lines and exited by the Railway Inn and carried on in the same direction until we reached the Teddington Gate entrance to Bushy Park.

On entering the park we were faced with the majestic view down Chestnut Avenue.

*

My phone informs me that this impressive mile long avenue was conceived by Sir Christopher Wren as a formal approach to Hampton Court Palace in the reign of William III & Mary II (1689-1702). Flanked on both sides by a single row of horse chestnuts and four rows of limes, the entrance at Teddington Gate provides the most striking view of the Avenue, with the 'Diana' Fountain and the Banqueting Hall as the backdrop.

Bushy Park is the second largest of the capital's eight Royal Parks and you can walk for miles in all directions. It is a fantastic place to enjoy the wildlife with roaming herds of Red and Fallow Deer. But beware, the deer are wild animals, and stags can become very aggressive. Just because they look cute and wander peacefully amongst you, don't forget that they are all around and sometimes only yards away and they can cover that ground in next to no time. Well faster than you can anyway.

Further inquisition of my phone revealed some helpful advice given by The Guardian on-line:

Titled: "What do you do if a deer goes for you?"

It states:

"Four incidents in the Royal Parks of Richmond and Bushy over the past fortnight have seen two visitors hospitalised. This is the rut, when stags and younger bucks, forget to eat, grow mean antlers and, half-starved, hormone-crazed and highly irritable, spend their days picking fights with one another.

So what's the best tactic if a stag sets his sights on you?

A trustee director of the British Deer Society, thinks that the problem in parks is that the deer are no longer frightened of the people, and the people are way too inquisitive about the deer.

"If you are attacked, climbing a tree is your best bet," she says. "Because if he's decided to go for you, he'll go for you. Run and he'll chase; curl up and he'll attack you on the ground."

I think that informed advice seems to comes with a few problems, as highlighted by a couple of comments about the article posted on-line.

I quote "daffydowndilly", who says:

Climb a tree, yes right ....and if there isn't one?

And, I think that the funniest comment (if not a bit cruel) comes from "WelshPaul", who says:

The best advice is to go with a slower, fatter, friend.

*

Armed with this information we started to walk down the avenue, and immediately were faced with a guy dancing around a tree, in the opposite direction of an aggressive looking stag, running around in this direction and then that trying to escape the stag. The comedy of the situation was quickly brought to earth by the look of terror on his face. We immediately wanted to help but didn't know what to do. Did this justify a 999 call? Before we could decide on a course of action, a pickup truck came out of a track on our right and headed straight for them. The driver headed to the right of the tree and placed the truck between the stag and the terrified man. The passenger door opened and the grateful guy quickly climbed in. The truck then headed off and disappeared up the avenue.

Shocked and unsure of we just witnessed, we stopped and stared. The stag, now deprived of it's victim, fixed it's stare on us. It seemed to have our scent. There were loads of people and deer in the park. All seemed to be going about their day and not bothering each other, but this stag had us firmly in it's sights. We started to walk to the left and around the stag, but then it made a couple of steps towards us. We froze. Those pubs that we passed now seemed much more appealing than continuing our walk through the park. Careful not to move suddenly or run we cautiously backed up towards entrance to the park. The stag glared and looked like it was about to attack. When we were near the gate, we couldn't control ourselves any more and we bolted through it and across the road outside. Relieved, to escape the attention of the stag, we walked back to Teddington feeling in need of a drink or two. We started at the first pub we came to which was the Railway Inn near the station.

As we sat down with our drinks, I chuckled to myself and my partner asked what was amusing me and I replied,

'I told you that you shouldn't buy that expensive perfume you are wearing, it's obviously far too dear!'

'No seriously, do you actually think that had anything to with it?' she questioned.

'I have no idea my dear, you will have to ask the deer. Another drink sweetheart?'

'Why not.'

HIGH DINING

We took our seats near the window, which was a long wall of glass. The lighting in the bar was complicated, subdued in the centre, contrasting the sunlight coming through the windows. There were many large and intricate chandeliers made from coloured glass and chains of glass beads hung from ceiling to floor around the windows and around the balustrade leading to the stairs and they sparkled in the sunlight. A large circular ceiling light consisted of hundreds of vertical wine bottles, containing coloured glass nuggets, which were illuminated from above. Very dimmed lights were inset into the wood stripped ceiling and long low hung downlighters added to the pleasing effect. Eye-catching modern artwork that was painted like colourful graffiti straight onto the walls, added a shabby chic feeling to the dazzling surroundings. The bar was central to the room and arrays of bottles of all shapes and sizes were lit invitingly. The barmen were busy shaking cocktails and the total effect was of rich elegance, radiating a warm welcome and a sense of luxury.

The ambiance of the place made me conscious of my own appearance and I questioned whether I should have made more of an effort and not worn jeans. But, studying the people around me reassured me that dress was casual and varied, with Kaftans and Burkas and plenty of jeans. However, some of the jeans looked like the deliberately faded designer type, whereas mine, were more Marks and Sparks, and just faded. The waiter came over and pleasantly took our pre-lunch drinks order and promptly delivered them to our table. We relaxed with our drinks and took in the amazing view. We stared in awe at the amazing pointed roof of the Gherkin vast in our eyeline and just fifty yards away. The views over London were breathtaking, the Shard glinted in the sunshine and as you looked down on the Gherkin, Tower Bridge appeared so far below us, it seemed like a tiny model replica of itself.

We were in a restaurant, at the top of the Heron Tower, which proclaims to be the highest dining experience in the U.K.
And an experience it certainly is.

My thoughts returned to our arrival earlier. Stepping straight off the busy city pavement through the entrance doors, we were immediately greeted and asked to confirm our reservations. We were subject to a security scan and body search and the contents of my partner's handbag were examined, before we were shown to the lift.

One impessive lift. Made of glass, it clung to the outside of the building and propelled us the the fortieth floor in just forty seconds. I thought, that if it went down any faster than it came up, we would probably experience weightlessness. I am glad I filmed it on my phone, as it is a memory well worth re-living.

Back in the bar, our trance-like state, induced by the panoramic views over the city from the fortieth floor, was interrupted by a waitress announcing that our table was ready.
As she led us into the impressive restaurant, that featured three walls of sheer glass, I felt a nervous anticipation that we would be taken to a table in the centre or towards or the back of the room, but our table was at the front, next to the centre window, which couldn't be better. Our menus were presented to us and I requested the wine list. A very comprehensive list with a great selection of wines from so many countries that it took some time to absorb. A quick scan however, revealed that there was nothing much costing under forty pounds and many were several hundreds of pounds. I was determined that this was not going to stop me ordering a good wine that we would enjoy, justifying it to myself with the thought that I don't do this everyday and I going to make the most of the occasion. We took our time pondering the menu and studying the wine list. When we ordered our

meals, I selected our wine, choosing what I thought was a good region and vintage. The wine waiter confirming that it was an excellent choice. Well, he is hardly going to say otherwise, is he? The wine tasting ritual was performed with much theatre; lots of wine swirling, holding to the light, more swirling, a bit of sniffing, more swirling and the eventual tasting and declaring it fit to drink.

We came for a late, leisurely lunch and we enjoyed the afternoon and early evening. We managed three courses and extended the day with plenty to drink. We watched the sun disappear behind the London skyline and the lights come on all over the city and and we agreed that this was an experience worth having.

*

In fact, I was so affected by the day, that I relived the experience in a dream. I dreamt that we were taking friends there for lunch. We were sure they would enjoy it as much as we did and be suitably impressed with our choice. As we entered the Heron Tower, I was really excited to see their reaction to the glass lift. Then the doorman, apologising profusely and hoping it wouldn't detract from our meal, announced that the lift was out of order and could we take the stairs.

***

IMAGINE A NUMBER

The other day, I asked my partner to imagine a number.

"Forty three million," she replied. "What's that?" I said. "This weeks lottery roll-over," she replied. "I can imagine that!"
"No, what I meant is an imaginary number. A number that doesn't exist, but can be expressed. For example; the square root of minus one is an imaginary number". At this point, she rather rudely suggested that I would be better off discussing this with my imaginary friend and she suddenly found the overwhelming urge to hoover the lounge.

But that's the problem, some people can have no imagination.

Unlike you, my readers. I am sure that you are imaginative, clever and curious.

I want you to imagine a number. An imaginary number. Lets start with one. That's easy, you can picture one. You know what it means. I am only going to have one. Just the one now. You use it all the time. If you multiply one by one, you get one, therefore the square root of one is one.

Then there is minus one. Still a simple concept you frequently use. It's freezing outside, it's minus one. If you multiply minus one, by minus one you also get one, therefore the square root of one is minus one.

But hang on, we have already said that the square root of one is one. Therefore, there are two answers; plus or minus the square root of one.

But there can't be any such number as the square root of minus one, because, as we said; if you multiply minus one by minus one you get plus one. So the square root of minus one is an imaginary number and we can express it as "i". But the fascinating thing is, if you put "i", an imaginary number, to the power of itself, you get back to a real number of minus one. We can write an imaginary number as a real number "b" multiplied by the imaginary unit "i", which is defined by its property; "i squared equals minus one". Thus, the square of an imaginary number bi is minus b squared. For example, 5i is an imaginary number and its square is minus twenty five.

I can tell that you are all enraptured and enthralled by all this, so I am sorry to tell you, that's all I have for now.

But don't worry, you will soon be able to read my follow up article entitled   "Having fun with differential calculus".

CEDRIC

Paul was on his knees praying, 'Oh god, I know I am not religious, I apologise for never going to church, but please can you help me with this one small problem.'

But before Paul could seek any more ecclesiastical advice, Jenny arrived home.

Paul decided that the best thing to do was share the problem with his loving wife. Jenny stared at him and as Paul struggled to translate her expression, she exploded,

'You are joking me?' she excaimed.
'No. She was desperate.' Paul said.
'She's nuts. You said so. She is a batty old lady. You call her the old bat next door.'
'Anyway. Sorry and all that, but Cedric is staying with us for now.'
'I can't leave you alone for a moment. How long is now? Why didn't you call me?'
'I did, but your phone went to voicemail, as usual. Why don't you ever answer the bloody thing?'

'Where is he now?'
'He is in our bedroom.'
'What. Why did you put him in there?'
'I don't know, but that's where he is okay!'

'So, where is Gaynor now?'
'Probably on a plane heading for Alicante.'
'What already?'
'I told you she was desperate. Sheila said that she would have Cedric, but then bailed at the very last moment. What could I do? It will be fine, it's only for a week.'

*

Paul was grateful that Jenny had reacted more favourably than he had anticipated and seemed to have calmed a little and accepted the situation. He had always referred to Gaynor as a stupid old bat, but had some sympathy there, as he couldn't help but compare her with his own ageing and mortality. He would be there one day. Probably one day sooner than he dread think. Now they had to look after Cedric for a week and the first thing he had to do was get him out of their bedroom and decide where to put him.

'Cedric, I have decided to put you in the lounge for now.'
'Cedric is a pretty boy. Hello Gaynor What's for tea?' squawked Cedric.
'Cedric. You are are a pretty boy. Unlike your

owner, Gaynor who is a stupid old bat.'
>'Stupid old bat,' squawked Cedric.
>'You got it Cedric,' answered Paul.
>'Stupid old bat.'
>'Yes. Thank you Cedric. We all know.'

*

Paul and Cedric were are becoming very attached. They would chat away and Cedric would perch on Paul's shoulder and they would watch TV together.
Jenny was becoming concerned. It is now only two days until Gaynor is due back from Spain and Paul has completely lost the plot. He is continually talking to Cedric and all Cedric keeps saying is 'stupid old bat. Gaynor is a stupid old bat.' Paul is trying to stop him but the more he tries to distract Cedric and and tells him not to say it, the more Cedric enjoys it.

>'Stupid old bat. Gaynor is a stupid old bat.'
>'What the hell are we going to do?' gasped Paul. 'Gaynor is due back in a couple of days and all this fucking parrot can say is Gaynor is a stupid old bat.'
>'Who's fault is that?'
>'Yes okay. I know. Thanks for your support, but what are we going to do?'
>'I think that the parrot gets it,' announced Jenny.
>'What?'
>' You heard me. You are going to have to kill

Cedric!'

'No, I can't do that.'

'For gods sake, of course you can. You are nearly six feet tall and Cedric barely eighteen inches. He shouldn't put up too much of a fight.'

'No, I meant, I can't just kill the poor thing.'

'Okay then, Gaynor will probably kill you when she gets back. If it was me to choose between Gaynor and the parrot. I know who I would choose.'

'No there must be another way,' pleaded Paul.

'What do have in mind exactly?'

'Henry!'

'What, as in Henry, next door's cat.'

'Exactly.'

'He is always hanging around, so we will entice him in with food.'

'Then what?'

'Don't be stupid. Then we will introduce him to Cedric.'

*

Henry was enjoying his steak dinner in the kitchen as Paul closed the back door and Jenny opened the door to the lounge. Leaving Henry to enjoy his meal, they went into the lounge and opened Cedric's cage. Cedric flew onto the back of the settee reciting 'Gaynor is a stupid old bat'. Henry, after polishing off his dinner, wandered into the lounge to see what all the noise was about. Then they saw each other. Cedric went silent and Henry prepared to ready to pounce. Cedric shrieked and flew straight at Henry with claws aimed at his head, Henry fled so fast as to leave a blurred image of him as he scuttled first to the closed kitchen door and then out of the door to the hall and up the stairs leaving a nasty deposit on the carpet behind him.

'That worked then,' gloated Jenny ' and your next brilliant idea?'
Paul said nothing, he just stormed across the lounge and opened the window, he then grabbed Cedric, who was still squawking 'Gaynor is a stupid old bat,' and threw him out the window and shut it behind him. 'We'll just have to say that he escaped.'

*

But Cedric didn't fly off . He just sat on the windowsill, pecking at the glass all afternoon and evening until Paul eventually gave up, opened the window and let Cedric back in.

'Back to square one then,' mocked Jenny.

'We'll just have to take him further from home. There is a wooded area at the back of the park. We'll take him there. We'll do it tomorrow,' declared Paul.

*

The next day Paul and Jenny took Cedric to the trees by the park. Being in the Twickenham area, there were many other small green parrots living wild in the trees, so Paul thought that Cedric would be fine. At least that is how he justified it to Jenny.

Looking to see that there that there was no one around Paul quickly got Cedric out of his cage and threw him up into a tree. Leaving a bemused Cedric perched on a branch. They retreated to the car and drove home. The journey home was spent in guilty silence after Paul had tried to justify himself and reassure them that Cedric would be okay and people shouldn't keep birds in a cage. It was cruel. Cedric would be happy now.

*

Paul's phoned pinged. It was a text from Gaynor saying that she had a great holiday and was home. She thanked them for looking after Cedric and said she would be around to collect him in about half an hour.
Paul and Jenny braced themselves and agreed on the story of how Cedric accidentally escaped. They put Cedric's cage out of sight.
The doorbell rang and they opened the door to an amazingly happy Gloria who was so grateful to them for looking after Cedric and she was overwhelmed with emotion that because of them, she had relaxed and enjoyed her holiday knowing that Cedric was in such safe hands. Paul and Jenny smiled and showed her into the lounge and seated her on the settee by the window. Paul asked her if she would like a drink, 'Tea, coffee or something stronger?'
 She said, 'a tea would be nice, thank you' and Jenny went into the kitchen to make it. Paul sat opposite

Gaynor looking at her seriously and started to explain, when he saw through the window behind Gaynor, Cedric land on the windowsill. Gaynor didn't immediately notice the horrified look on Paul's face, but then Jenny returned to the room with the cup of tea, and froze as she stared at the window. Gaynor looked around. Confused she exclaimed, 'Cedric, what are you doing out there?' She rushed and opened the window and Cedric flew in. Instantly recognising her Cedric flew to Gaynor and perched on her shoulder, lovingly nibbling her ear.

Then he squawked loudly; 'Stupid old bat. Gaynor is a stupid old bat.'

***

YOU HAVE CONTROL

The reassuring silence of the country. There are fields and hedge rows are all around us, as far as the eye can see. An idyllic, quiet country scene on a sunny day. Then the silence is rudely broken by an unidentified distant buzzing noise. The noise becomes louder, as a Cessna appears, from behind a row of trees and ascends in to the clear blue sky.

The plane is owned by Robin, who despite being middle-aged, lives in the fast lane of life. He is successful, confident and loud. He is wearing crystal belted designer jeans and white open necked shirt, complemented by hand tooled cowboy boots. He is in the captain's seat flying the Cessna and beside him is his friend Paul who is about the same age and wearing jeans and a t-shirt. Sitting behind them are their respective wives: Karen, wearing bright red chinos with pink suede wedges and an off-the-shoulder white t-shirt and numerous gold necklaces, clutching a Mulberry handbag and Jenny, who is wearing white cropped skinny jeans and an orange t-shirt.

Robin is talking to Paul through headphones;
"What do you think Paul, isn't this just a perfect day for flying. We are just coming up over your house. There it is. Look."
Robin banks the plane so Paul can see it.
"Yes, I got it. A great view of it. I'm glad I cleaned the pool it looks good from up here. I wish I'd brought a camera now."
Paul turns around to Jenny, and shouts to her;
"Look there's our house."
Jenny shouts back against the noise of the engines;
"That's where I should be". It took some persuading on Paul's part to get Jenny to come up in the plane today and she is not exactly thrilled.
Karen laughs and tells Jenny; "You'll be fine. It's perfectly safe."

Paul is really enjoying the flight; "What a day for it" he exclaims, "This is just great. You know, if I was to come back in another life, I'd like to come back as a bird."
"You think there's an after life?," Robin questions.
"No I don't believe in anything. Well nothing religious or spiritual anyway. Do you?"
"Me. No mate, no I don't believe. The only thing I believe in is me. In this life no-one is going to look after you better than yourself. You got one shot at it, make the most of it. Have fun."

"You have control." Robin says suddenly handing

control of the plane to Paul.
Paul is surprised and stammers; "What. Oh yeah. I have control."

Paul takes over the controls of the plane and gets the feel of it. He practices a turn to the left and a turn to the right and then tries a small descent followed by a long gentle climb up to 4000 feet.
"Feels all right? " asks Robin.
"Feels great." says Paul. "More power than I am used to. Thanks."
"What do you you fancy doing, Paul?"
"I'd like to swoop down and dip the wheels in the sea and then soar back into the sky like a bird!"
"I don't know about that mate, but you can try a long dive and pull up into a climb."
Paul needs no more encouragement and starts his dive, just as Jenny taps Robin on the shoulder and he turns rounds to her and peels off one of his earphones to listen to her.
Jenny is getting uncomfortable and asks Robin; "Why can't we just fly smoothly."
She is shocked and scared when Robin tells her; "It's not me. Your husband is flying the plane."
Jenny shouts; "Oh my God, no please, he's only had three lessons."
Robin just laughs; "He will be fine."

Robin turns back to the front and Paul is diving rapidly as groans come from the back. Robin is suddenly concerned, but keeps cool and calmly tells

Paul to watch his airspeed.
Paul glances at the instruments and goes for the throttle. The sea is coming towards him faster than he envisaged.

"No, don't do that," Robin said, more abruptly than he intended, "Raise your nose."

Paul obeys. He is worried and would gladly hand the controls back to Robin, but pride prevents him from doing so until Robin tells him to.

Robin is starting to raise his voice and his normal, cool calm, laid back attitude is showing an touch of anxiety;

"Full power. Pull your nose up more.... More."

The Cessna gets closer to the sea than anyone wanted. Much too close. There is a worrying moment as it levels, some ten feet above the sea and then ascends.
Robin quickly regains his cool and lightly quips;
"Nearly got to dip them wheels then!"
Paul lets out the breath he was holding; "Shit! Sorry" he gasps.
"No worries." says Robin, now calm and back to his old confident self; "Just a bit of fun! Mate. Although I don't think Jenny appreciated it."

Jenny is now screaming; "That's it! Take me back. I want to go back. You are both mad. Paul, what the hell are you doing? Are you trying to kill us all? Robin you are just as bad for letting him."

Karen knows better than to try and humour Jenny now and tells Robin that she thinks it's time for home.

Paul is hiding the fact that he is somewhat relieved to hand control back to Robin; "You have control"

"I have control. We'll head back now then shall we." laughs Robin.

After a smooth and event free landing. They taxi to a parking area near the club house and park up. Paul helps Karen and Jenny out of the plane while Robin is busy doing last checks and ensuring that everything is switched off and correctly stowed. The mood is now happy, all being safely back on terra firma.

Robin jumps down from the plane and comes over to them. He jokingly drops to his knees, bends forward and kisses the ground.

Paul shouts to Robin; "And you told me you didn't believe."

Robin replies with a smile; "I don't mate. I am just worshipping the ground that I walk on."

UNSEEN REVENGE

There he was, large as life, standing no more than than ten feet away from me. Robin Fraser. Robin by name. Robbing by nature. He had just pulled up in the car park and was getting out of his car, when I spotted him. He had a brand new, top of the range BMW….. flash git. I had probably paid for that, I thought. I intensely hated Robin, because he had cheated me out of nearly forty thousand pounds. My company had done a lot of work for his company and was owed the money, when Robin pulled the plug on it. His company was supposed to be in financial difficulty and had become insolvent, but we all new it was a deliberate ploy to rid himself of half a million pounds worth of creditors. He was up and trading with a new company within days and we couldn't get him or our money. He had done nothing illegal according to the laws of limited liability.

Robin was standing by his car staring at young lady, who was bent over her supermarket trolley rearranging her shopping. His eyes were obviously focussed on her backside. I also looked at her and have to confess, that I could understand why it was a source of such attraction. She was quite stunning. Absolutely beautiful with a slim figure. How she got into those tight jeans, just defied the imagination.

I quickly hatched a plan to upset Robin's day. I walked over to where she was still bent over her trolley and gave her bum a friendly stroke! She jumped around and saw no-one near, except for Robin who was leering down at her. She screamed, "what's your game, you pervert?" Then she gave him an almighty slap across the face. Robin recoiled in confusion. "What's wrong with you, you psycho bitch?" he shouted. She was obviously the highly strung type and shrieked as loud as she could "Help, help, somebody help me, I am being attacked by a pervert." Robin looked very scared. He tried to calm her, but she was having none of it and kept shouting hysterically. I could see that Robin was about to do a runner. He headed for his car. I was just there, by him and I put out a helping foot. Robin tripped over it and fell headlong into her trolley full of groceries, propelling down the side of his car, nicely modifying the paintwork.

I was having a great time and I thought it couldn't get any better, until a car stopped just by us and out popped PC plod and WPC plod. How good was that. What brilliant timing, I thought. They couldn't fail to notice the disturbance and were quick to intervene. What a scene. Robin was ranting and she was screaming. Our Police duo tried to calm the situation and said they would listen to them, one at a time and for them to both stop shouting. They turned to Robin first who said "She is completely mad. I've done nothing. She attacked me completely with out reason and has vandalised my car". Then they turned to her as she shouted, "He's lying, he attacked me. I was leaning over my trolley and he came up behind me and grabbed my arse. He's some sort of dangerous pervert and I didn't touch his car. He did it. He's the one that's off his trolley."

I didn't know who they would believe, they both sounded crazy. So, as their attention was on her and away from Robin, I decided to give her case a helping hand. With Robin standing just behind the police, I moved in and gave the WPC's behind a gentle squeeze. It worked a treat. Out came the handcuffs and despite Robin persistently protesting his innocence, he was bundled into the back of the police car. Oh such joy!

I know that I shouldn't abuse my super power, but sometimes it can be great fun being invisible.

***

DAMAGED

Charles walked into his walk in shower.
Self satisfied with the size of his new shower. He thought to himself that you could have six people in here easily, perhaps ten or more. Counting the floor tiles made up of 18 inch squares, he calculated that if he allocated one tile to a person and there was three tiles wide and six and a half long, he could share his shower with another eighteen and a half people. But then he thought that six would be enough. Probably three couples. No, perhaps too many. Four would be better. Ah, but is that two women and two men? No, he didn't like the sound of that. How about him and three women, that sounded good. But what if they were lesbians. No, that wouldn't do, or would it, he had these fantasies about lesbians and it might be fun, but would he feel ignored.

Charles was easily distracted from reality and drifted on the edge of life in a half fantasy world most of the time. Charles didn't like reality. From an early age he was made to feel inadequate. His mother criticised his every move. He felt a failure in her eyes in whatever he tried to do.

Just as he started to shower, he noticed a small woodlouse clinging to the wall tiles. He couldn't share his shower with a woodlouse, however small it was. He took the shower head and gently washed it down the drain. He felt guilty, he never wanted to kill anything and hoped the woodlouse survived and happily swam out to wherever wood lice swim to.

Overcoming his guilt and with a dreaded feeling of karma, he soaked his head and shampooed his hair. Eyes closed, he massaged his scalp and enjoyed the relaxing feeling of the warm water washing over his body.

Below, in the darkness and unknown to Charles, the woodlouse had survived, as he wished. It had found a ledge to cling to, just under the drain and it had increased in size. Only half a centimetre when it was washed away, it was now nearly an inch long and had managed to squeeze up through the drain back into the shower. Nourished by the warm water and shampoo, it grew to six inches and then a foot and continued to grow rapidly.

Charles was oblivious, shampooing his hair with eyes closed and warm water flowing over his shoulders, relaxed and content, enjoying the pleasant sensation.

Woody was now over three foot long and growing

at a fantastic rate. He grew and grew and was about nine feet tall, and taking up most of the shower, when Charles, after rinsing his hair and face, opened his eyes and staring into the vast mouth of this leggy monster was overwhelmed with fear. Terrified, he screamed and jumped up and with flailing arms, smacked his wife in the face.

'Aow. What the fuck,' she cried as Charles came back to reality.

'Sorry. So sorry. I didn't mean to hit you.'

'Charles. Not again. How many more times? What goes on inside your head? I've tried, but and can't take it any more. Whatever planet you live on. I don't want to be there. I have had enough and please don't go through your pleadings that it will never happen again. It does and it keeps happening. Charles, that's it. I am leaving you and please do one last thing for me. Tell your bitch of a Mother that she is the mother in law from hell and she is an insane, she is a evil cow and is probably the cause of all your problems and you really have a lot of problems. I am finished with you and your crazy family.'

NOTHING

I want to talk about nothing. That does not mean that I have nothing to say to you. But, how do you describe nothing. Are you aware that there is nothing, or does that imply that you are aware of something?
Dust to dust, ashes to ashes. When you are dead, you are dead. Or are you?
"Believe in me and you shall live forever," I hear told.

Wouldn't it be nice and easy to believe in life after death. It's especially at times like this, solitary in the darkness and awake in the early hours of the morning, when dark thoughts enter my head, that I would like to believe, but I don't.

I remember a couple of close friends that died young.
Kevin introduced me to flying. He was a real inspiration, exciting to be with, a real ball of energy. He lived his life in the fast lane. Then, without warning, suddenly dropped dead. He was in his forties.

Brian was my best man at my wedding. He loved to party and was full of life. We shared many crazy adventures. He died of cancer aged 56.

If there is a life after death, I am sure that they would have contacted me. They haven't.

I think death is final. What we have to lose is unimaginable.
But lose it, we will. Nothing is a really hard thing to comprehend.

Putting it selfishly: when there is no me, there is nothing, Nothing for me. The thought of dying haunts me.

They say life is not a rehearsal.
So we should get on with the show.
Because, when there is nothing.
There is nothing
Nothing is forever.

I am sorry, but I have no good ending for this tale. No real conclusion, Just nothing in the end.

LIVING IN LANZAROTE

Every-time I see it, I wonder that it is still there, still standing and intact. No plane has landed on it yet. A testimony to the safety of air travel. The planes seem to skim it's roof daily, without incident. When we get out out of the car to do the weekly shop, I fight the urge to duck as another plane flies over the car park. At one end the runway at Arrecife Airport, there is the Atlantic Ocean and at the other is HiperDino. This is our Supermarket of choice. Think of a large Tescos with wider aisles, fewer people and background music. A pleasurable shopping experience, if there is such a thing, with an added bonus for plane spotters! But beware, although not affected by siestas and open on Sundays, at the hint of a Fiesta, it is shut, so know your Fiesta calender before going there.

Driving there is easy, heading west, you just drop off the LZ-2 onto a slip road. Although this section of the LZ-2 is the busiest road on the island, it is easy to navigate. Driving home, however, is more of a challenge, as you go under the main highway, via the dreaded Roper's roundabout which has six exits and multiple lanes. It is busy and fast moving and it interconnects to another roundabout. It is not for the faint hearted.

I remember, when I used to regularly drive in London in busy, congested traffic, I quickly learned techniques to carve through the traffic. One method is the blinkered approach, which is especially effective in dealing with London Cabbies. Where there are two cars and one space, head for that space, but stare straight ahead and don't show any awareness of the car beside you also heading for that space, do not hesitate, do not falter, just slowly edge in. Now, if your adversary is a London cab driver, he will have seen you, but don't show that you have seen him. He will not instantly give way, it is not in his nature, he is a London cab driver. Just keep going and don't look round, even though you are convinced you might be hearing the scrape of bodywork any second soon. Have faith. He will not hit you, he is a professional driver. Keep your nerve and you will win the space. You know when you have it, by the friendly banter emitting from the cab window.

Anyway, I digress. Back to Ropers roundabout. Definitely, do not use this technique here. They are likely to hit you and frequently do, judging by the number of dents on the locals cars. There are different rules here. First and most important. Don't stop, unless you are actually about to drive into something. This especially applies when entering the roundabout. If there is the slightest gap go for it. If you stop, you will be bogged down for ages. Second: be prepared to swerve quickly, either left or right, wherever there is a gap, or to avoid collision. Third: ignore lanes, there is no lane control here and right of way is merely perceived. Lastly: don't, whatever you do, signal, that gives away your intentions and leaves you at a disadvantage. Just take the shortest route to your exit.

After that, the journey home is relatively simple. Take the circunvalacion that goes north around Arrecife and take the turn off to Tahiche, where you pass the Cesar Manrique Foundation, turn right to Guatiza, pass the windmill at the Cactus Garden and then turn towards the coast on a small track through the cactus fields, that leads to Charco del Palo. We lived in Charco for six months in 2007/2008. We were welcomed by locals and enjoyed our time in the village. For such a tiny place, it had many facilities including three restaurants, a Pub, a shop and a hairdressers. Our favourite restaurant was La Tunera which served great food at reasonable Spanish prices. Pete's Pub was also good and where you would find a few ex-pats.

The first time I introduced my partner to Charco, we had a drink in the restaurante Romantica and sat by a window overlooking the sea. A couple walked past our window and caught her attention, she was shocked and accidentally knocked a glass of wine from the table. She spotted the man proudly displaying his willy ornament. Perhaps, I should have warned her that it was "a clothes optional village".

I was a regular visitor to the Island. The first time I discovered it was in the early nineteen eighties and then it was so different to today. The Gran Hotel in Arrecife and the five mile strip of shops, bars and restaurants in Puerto del Carmen just didn't exist. The building that is now the 5 star Gran in Arrecife was constructed in 1988 in contravention of strict building regulations that did not allow any buildings above the height of a palm tree. That's three storeys maximum, but most buildings were restricted to just one or two stories thanks to the inspired thinking of Cesar Manrique, who contributed so much to preserve the unique qualities of the Island. Construction of the seventeen storey high rise monster was stopped. It remained empty until 1990 when a fire gutted it. The burnt out eyesore of a high-rise shell remained for over ten years, as it was too difficult to demolish. Arguments as to what to do with it continued, until finally, when a developer approached the Cabildo to propose completion of the building as a five star luxury hotel, permission was granted. The building work took several years to complete and cost 26 million euros. It was opened in July 2004. Today, there is a bar and a restaurant at the top of the hotel with superb views over the sea, Reducto beach and the city. It is well worth a visit. If you are driving, park your car in the underground car park. Go to the back of the car park where it is nearest the coast and go through a large steel door. There is no sign on the door, but do not be deterred, go down the corridor and turn right where it leads to a lift. Select floor seventeen. Initially you see nothing but darkness, but then it rises up into the sunlight, and you realise it is glass sided and you take in the fantastic views as it rises to the restaurant. Relax over a great meal and a glass or two of wine, It's a pleasant way to spend an afternoon, taking in the views from the top of the only high rise building in Lanzarote.

I love Lanzarote and really enjoyed living there. I don't go there as often as I used to. It's not the same visiting a place where you used to live. When I returned to the Island a few years ago, a lot had changed. The bookshop where we used to go for our weekly book club meetings had closed, one of our favourite restaurants in Costa Teguise was empty. A lot of the bars and restaurants that were owned by friends had changed hands and a lot of our British friends had returned to the UK.
Sadly the Restaurante Romantica in Charco is now a ruin and unlikely to be rebuilt and La Tunera is closed.

The financial collapse of 2008 hit Lanzarote badly, but after my more recent visit in February 2020, I felt, thankfully, that things are improving.

But now Coronavirus has again damaged tourism on the island even though Lanzarote has some of the lowest infection rates in the world and only a low number of deaths.

***

LOST CHILDHOOD

A droplet of blood fell on the warm brown sand. The boy was gripping a large conch shell with such intensity, he didn't notice that the edge of the shell had cut into his fingers. The beach, on which he was sitting, was not exactly the white sands of the Caribbean. It was dirty brown with clumps of grass and vegetation, but it was quiet. He often came to sit out here to get away from the frustration of his daily life. He would sit alone, solitary rather than lonely, because to be lonely, you had to be missing friends. This boy had never known many friends and there were no kids of his age and kind here. He hated it here. His Father constantly complained that he just moped around and showed no interest in anything and spent most of his time hanging around with the servants. He said that we were lucky to be here in Ancon, there were plenty of things for him to do and he should appreciate that this was so much better and safer than Aberdan, where they lived before.

The boy couldn't remember Aberdan. How could he? He was only six weeks old when he flew from Northolt Aerodrome with his Mother, to join his Father in Aberdan and only aged two, when they hurriedly flew out again, evicted by the government. His Father firmly putting the blame on Mohammed Mosaddegh, who he said, was a money grabbing thief.

The fact of the matter being that he was the democratically elected Prime Minister of Persia and in the spring of 1952, he nationalised the oil industry and the Anglo-Iranian Oil Company's refinery where his Father worked. It was the Brit's expertise that built the largest oil refinery in the world, but is was the Persians' oil and Mosaddegh wanted it back.

It caused a bit of an upset and Clement Attlee, initially mobilised the British military, but then settled on an embargo of the Aberdan refinery by the Royal Navy. The Americans who smelt oil, allied themselves with Britain and the CIA and MI5 jointly orchestrated a Coup to bring down and replace Mosaddegh. There was a violent uprising in Aberdan and hundreds of people were killed, including one of his Father's friends, who was shot. They were evacuated in an American military plane, with no time to take any possessions or say good-byes.

The boy on the beach gazed out to sea and watched another oil tanker slowly disappear over the horizon, as he had watched so many before. He dreamed that he was on it and travelling to a happier place. He longed for a home he did not know. He had no real memories of anywhere else but still felt that there must be somewhere better than here.

Carlos spotted the boy and approached him. Speaking Spanish, Carlos told the boy that he was wanted in the house as his parents had some news for him. The boy responded in Spanish. Speaking Spanish came easily to him, without the need to mentally translate, as he had spoken it for nearly a third of his life. He asked Carlos if it was good or bad news, but Carlos didn't know and steered him towards the house just down the beach.

Carlos and his wife, Maria, lived in part of his parent's large wooden, single story house. They were both in their mid twenties. Carlos did all the jobs around the house and looked after the grounds and the animals and Maria cleaned and cooked. The part of the house that over-lapped the beach was built on wooden stilts and at very high tides, the sea would threaten to lap around them. A wooden veranda with fine wire mesh for windows surrounded two thirds of the house. The mesh would allow for ventilation and keep the insects out.

Carlos and the boy entered the lounge through the veranda and his Parents were sitting there talking to Maria. His Parents looked up at him and his Mother smiled and said,

"Good news we are going home."

They had first class tickets for a voyage on the Reina del Pacifico, which could accommodate 800 passengers and was part of the Pacific Steam Navigation Company's fleet. They were leaving Guayaquil next month, destined for Liverpool via the Panama canal.

The boy was over-joyed, hugged his Mother and then looked sadly towards Carlos and Maria. He wouldn't miss much, but he would miss them.

Home, they were going home at last. As they sailed away, the boy was up on deck and joyously waved goodbye to Ecuador. Later at dinner, the atmosphere was relaxed and happy. The boy really looking forward to better things to come. His Mother beaming. But then his Father, cautiously introducing the subject, started to tell us about the new oilfields in Libya and Iraq.

*

Today, nearly sixty years later, as I sit alone on this deserted beach, toying with a shell and contemplating life. I watch a distant oil tanker cross the horizon, silhouetted by the setting sun. It takes me back to that time. A time that I now have little or no memories of, as if some protective force has erased it from my brain and I realise sadly, that my childhood is missing.

***

Printed in Great Britain
by Amazon